THE GRAND TOURNAMENT

Written by DS SMITH

Illustrations by NEEDRA KRUSE

COPYRIGHT

The Grand Tournament, Book III of the *Jubilations of Dancia*.

ISBN 978-0-578-21752-9

Illustrations and Layout » Needra Kruse | www.ndkdesign.studio

Illustration Assistant » Justin Kruse

The art for this book was created using watercolor, pen, and marker. The effective date of copyright registration for this book's illustrations—by Needra Kruse and Justin Kruse—is 26 December 2018.

Interior Design/Typography » **HL Smith**

Editing » Andrea Vinley Converse | AndreaVinleyConverse.com

DEDICATION

I would like to dedicate this book to
my wise and wonderful wife, the sure
compass to my wild imaginings.

To my kids, whose love and laughter are
my deepest treasure.

And to my parents, for helping breathe life
into dreams.

- DS SMITH

To my dad who has been so generous with
his time, wisdom, and talent.

- NEEDRA KRUSE

SPEEDY AND SLOW, TO THE TOURNAMENT WE GO

Sweet lemon beams of sunshine drenched the candied land of Dancia. Lime whisper grass swayed as breezes darted this way and that. The air was full of the scent of Twirly-toe Tulias and orange Buttercup Blossoms. Sir Sylas the Speedy and his trusty horse, Slowpoke, laughed as the gentle air lifted the heat from their warm bodies. Not that they were working particularly hard.

Sylas was eyeballing those Twirly-toed Tulias. He asked Brie if he should pick a bouquet for his dear friend Ballerina Princess Illyana. They were her favorites. The little mouse Brie, half asleep on Slowpoke's back, gave Sylas a slow nod of her head.

Slowpoke thought he could hear patches of lime grass whisper to him, "Eat me, eat me!" He stretched his neck down to chomp the yummy greens.

Sylas, Slowpoke and Brie were on their way to Princess Illyana's palace. Brie had flown in the day before to invite Sir Sylas to the Grand Tournament (and to keep an eye on Slowpoke). Now they were on their way to compete in the annual Dancian games. The princess's palace was only a day away as the horse hoof steps, but Sylas had started the journey four days early. Slowpoke often took a long time to get anywhere.

"Ah, this is perfect weather for the tournament," Sylas said. "It's going to be so great to see Thurin and our friends: the princess, Sir Josef the Jolly and Natalia."

"Come on, Slowpoke." Sylas urged his beloved steed. "I can't wait to get to Princess Illyana's palace and beat Sir Josef in hedgehog bowling. That's my favorite part of the tournament," he said into Slowpoke's cocked ear. "I'm dancipating the look on Josef's face when I beat him again, just like I did last year."

"Neeigghh," replied Slowpoke as he sauntered down the road. "Illyana, goooood fuun."

When the sun had risen high above the giant's cloud stacks, Sylas called a halt. They were at the edge of Amble River and decided to cool down and eat the lunch that Sylas' guardian, Lady Veriona, had prepared. Sylas' thoughts drifted to the talk he'd had earlier that morning with her.

DANCIPATING:
THIS MEANS THAT YOU ARE
DANCING WITH ANTICIPATION

3

The food wise and chuckling duchess of Lavender's Valley was preparing tasty tidbits for their journey in her kitchen.

"You tell the princess that I grew these Coolcumbers especially for her. Give that dear girl a kiss on the cheek and a hug from me," Lady Veriona said.

"Wrapping these in Wintermint boughs will help them stay fresh. They should keep till you get to the palace. That is if you can get that horse of yours to move. Honestly Sylas, I don't know why you love that big lazy galoot so much."

"Now Aunt Veriona," Sylas protested, throwing his arms out. "I don't know why you're always picking on poor Slowpoke. He can run fast—when he wants to—which . . ." Sylas cleared his throat and mumbled, "I admit, isn't too often . . . but still, he's young."

"I know he is dear, so young, you all are." Lady Veriona paused a moment then handed a box to Sylas. "That's candied Wintermint bark for Thurin. I've missed your brother so, this past year, while he's been serving at the palace. He'll come back to me just as you did last year, all grown and strong, a squire! I'm so proud of you both."

"Thurin misses you too, Aunt Veriona," Sylas said, then held up the box. "And I know he's missed Wintermint bark."

Just then a big wave of water from Amble River splashed Sylas and washed away his daydream. He spluttered and blinked his eyes. There stood Slowpoke in the middle of the stream with his big horsey mouth curved in a grin.

"Did you do that Slowpoke?" Sylas asked his horse. "Did you splash me, you big stinker? Well, I guess that means I'm going to have to . . . GET YOU!"

Sylas sprang into the stream, cupping handfuls of water to splash at Slowpoke. Slowpoke jumped up and down causing water to fly everywhere.

Very soon they were both soaked amid lots of laughter and neighing, which scared away all the fish.

After they dried off, Sylas cast his line in the water hoping the fish would come back. Then he and Brie pulled out lunch and laid out a bag of oats for his horse.

Slowpoke wandered off, nose to the ground, sniffing for a little pre-lunch snack to prepare his tummy for some serious oat eating.

He hungrily munched on some grass, then a patch of clover, until he found a clump of Blue Bell Giggle Blossoms.

As the delighted Slowpoke began chomping the delicate blooms, he startled a little flower fairy who had been happily drinking Blue Bell nectar from one of the flowers. She rose up into the air, her tiny wings beating furiously.

She gave Slowpoke such a tongue lashing that the remaining Blue Bells hid their giggle blossoms. Then she zapped Slowpoke on his nose with her little wand of fairy fury. Poor Slowpoke whipped his head in the air, his nose stung and his eyes were watering.

Then he stopped. As his nose was pointed upward into the soft summer breeze, he smelled one of his favorite things in the world. . . CARROT CAKE! An excited whinny escaped his lips. Thereafter, he gave no mind to the fairy's scolding.

Ordinarily, Slowpoke didn't move fast, but a few things could make him move quickly. Carrot cake was one of those things. Faster than you can say, "Carrot cake for lunch," Slowpoke was galloping full speed down the road. The flower fairy, thinking Slowpoke was running from her, gave a final little fist shake and returned to her blossoms.

Slowpoke—fairies, flowers and oats forgotten—thundered like a battle stallion into the peaceful village of Meander. He followed his nose up the steps and right into the Lazy River Inn. There, Slowpoke started eating the very first slice of carrot cake he saw. Meanwhile, Sylas had woken from a little fishing nap and looked to feed some oats to his horse. But the sleepy squire couldn't find Slowpoke anywhere.

"Now where has that pokeylicious Slowpoke gotten to," Sylas wondered aloud. "He couldn't have gotten very far, as slow as he is. He never misses lunch, especially when lunch is oats." Just then, Sylas smelled something spicy and sweet. He knew right away why his habitually hungry horse had hurried off.

"Uh oh, I smell carrot cake. That means trouble!"

Hurriedly, Sylas grabbed his gear and with Brie on his shoulder headed toward that carrot cake smell. He hastened into the town of Meander where a great commotion— shouts and screams, the sound of breaking plates and high-pitched whinnies—were coming out of the Inn. Sylas didn't need to look hard to find his horse because he heard a very loud and frusticated voice say:

FRUSTICATED:
THIS MEANS YOU ARE SO FRUSTRATED THAT YOU ARE READY TO TAKE A VACATION FROM YOUR FRUSTRATIONS.

"BACK! BACK, You great equine beast!" Followed by . . .

"Get those horsey choppers off my carrot cake—" and then . . .

"Stop licking my icing!"

Then Sylas heard another loud whinny and saw Slowpoke run out of the Inn. His ears were tucked behind him, and his tail swished back and forth as he tried to protect his hindquarters. Right behind him, a chef barreled through the doorway, his chef's hat askew, whopping Slowpoke on his rump with a great big broom.

"STOP! WAIT!"
Sylas cried as he
ran up to Slowpoke.

Slowpoke was a sight to behold.
His cheeks bulged with carrot
cake. White cream covered his
long nose, face and ears. His tummy
was twice its normal size, loaded with
yummy cake. "Now look here, Slowpoke..." Sylas
started to say to his battered and frosted horse, when
the extremely excited chef interrupted him.

"My cakes . . . four of them . . . right off my patron's plates . . . he ate . . . why he just came right in . . . my cakes. . . HE ate . . . ALL of them!!!" the chef spluttered. He looked Slowpoke right in the eye and shook his finger, "YOU . . . You . . . you great big naughty, naughty . . . CAKE EATER!"

Sylas stepped in, stroking his wide-eyed horse on the neck. "Peace down, big fella. It's going to be ok." Sylas turned to the Chef. "I am so sorry, Master Chef. Forgive Slowpoke. You see, my hungry horse loves carrot cake. If anybody knows a good carrot cake, it's Slowpoke."

"Your cakes must be very fine indeed," continued Sylas, "to make my normally well behaved horse so intrusive. I will, of course, reimburse you for all your cakes and pay for your customer's lunches and any broken dishes."

INTRUSIVE:
TO INTRUDE IS TO FORCEFULLY PUT YOURSELF IN SOMEONE'S WAY OR IN SOMEONE'S SPACE. SLOWPOKE WAS DEFINITELY NOT WELCOME AT THE INN.

"Well, I do make the finest carrot cake in all the land," boasted the chef, somewhat calmer now that he was getting paid well for his trouble.

"Neeiiigghhh," Slowpoke said, "good caaakkke!"

Sylas gave the chef a chocolate gold coin, a generous sum for all the food. "But now, Slowpoke, my mischief making muncher," Sir Sylas said, "we must move on to Princess Illyana's tournament."

"Illyana?" Slowpoke asked. Visions of huge royal carrots danced in Slowpokes eyes. "Carrots? Garden?"

"Yes Slowpoke, Illyana's Royal Garden," Sylas said sternly. "But don't expect any carrots from her garden after the way you just behaved."

Poor Slowpoke was so sad about the possibility of not getting any royal carrots from the palace gardens that he lost his appetite and forgot to be pokey. With his ears hung low and Brie giving him a very long and serious talking to, the three arrived at Princess Illyana's pink rock candy palace the very next day.

LET THE GAMES BEGIN

The day of the Dancian tournament arrived. Sails and paddle craft filled Deep Water Lake. The town of Vigoratto was bursting with balloons, flowers, music, and people. Up above the town, vendors selling their wares lined the palace walls. Dancians full of good cheer were in the streets waving little flags and laughing, eating great big turkey legs and marzipan pigs. Children ran around playing. And everywhere, on high to down low, on tabletops and in the lanes, on walls and chairs—and sometimes even on each other—people danced. Oh, how the Dancians loved to dance. And how they adored Ballerina Princess Illyana, the finest dancer of them all.

While the friends waited for Princess Illyana, Sir Josef was finishing one of his unfortunate jokes. "So the sheep that's dressed in black says to the serving girl 'That's some baaaadd service!' " Josef looked at his friends. They stared back. "You get it, right? Baaaadd! It's a black sheep. Baaaa. Baaaaddd service!" Josef was laughing so hard at his own joke that he had to wipe a tear from his eye.

Sylas and Thurin just shook their heads at him. The brothers were leaning up against Slowpoke. Natalia gave Sir Josef the Jolly a small smile.

Finally, when Josef had stopped laughing, Sylas said, "Josef, that was a baaaad joke, even worse than usual. It was so bad I might have to bar you from telling any more jokes for the rest of the tournament."

Off in the distance, Princess Illyana stood atop a platform reunited with Brie, who was perched on her lace lined shoulder. Illyana was dressed in a royal purple gown and golden crown. In her excitement, Princess Illyana glided and pirouetted around the stage as she talked to a great crowd of attentive Dancians. The King and Queen were not in attendance this year as they waited for a new baby sister for Princess Illyana to arrive (at least the princess hoped it would be a baby sister.)

The friends could not hear what she was saying. But the crowd could, and they roared and cheered and clapped. The royal trumpets sounded. Then 10,000 balloons of every color were released to float up over the blueberry expanse of Deep Water Lake. There was a moment's hush. Then the crowd and everyone in the palace, in the streets, and on the rooftops of Vigarotto cheered. This concluded the commencement ceremony.

HAPPY TUTU!

COMMENCEMENT CEREMONY:
TO COMMENCE IS TO BEGIN OR START SOMETHING.
A COMMENCEMENT CEREMONY IS A
PARTY YOU HAVE TO GET THE PARTY STARTED.

Besides hedgehog bowling, the tournament hosted jousting, archery, bubble gum blowing, spicy pickle eating, licorice stick pole vaulting, craft competitions, a riddle tournament, a story telling and poetry contest, music and singing tryouts and dance-offs. The tournament would conclude with a grand ball in the blue crystal ballroom where Princess Illyana would perform a Saganspin, a traditional dance recounting the victories (and defeats) of the Grand Tournament.

For three days, the friends competed. Sir Sylas the Speedy showed everyone how fast he could shoot arrow snakes from his bow. The hungry little arrows loved flying from Sylas' bow because they usually landed in the vanilla center of the cherry swirl targets. Even the older knights who competed said Sir Sylas was a rare and gifted archer.

Sir Thurin the Mighty picked such a big juicy piece of bubble gum from the royal Chewy Tree that it took him three hours just to chew it soft. When it was finally soft enough to blow a bubble, he put his mighty lungs to work. He blew a bubble so big that the wind picked it up, with Thurin still attached to it, and blew that bubble up Up UP into the air. He blew right out over Deep Water Lake where the bubble popped and dropped Thurin straight down into the water with a big blueberry *kerplopp*. He was so far from shore that a paddleboat had to come pick him up out of the lake.

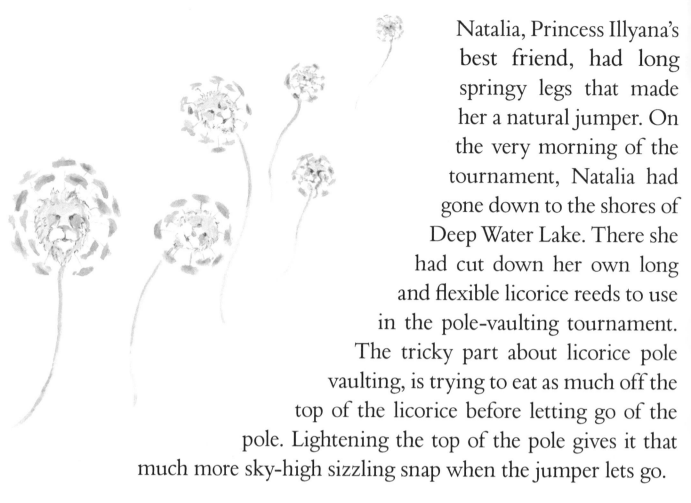

Natalia, Princess Illyana's best friend, had long springy legs that made her a natural jumper. On the very morning of the tournament, Natalia had gone down to the shores of Deep Water Lake. There she had cut down her own long and flexible licorice reeds to use in the pole-vaulting tournament. The tricky part about licorice pole vaulting, is trying to eat as much off the top of the licorice before letting go of the pole. Lightening the top of the pole gives it that much more sky-high sizzling snap when the jumper lets go.

She ran holding her licorice pole out in front of her and then jumped. The blue pole flexed almost in half. The crowd could see her eating that licorice as fast as she could. *Snap . . . twang*, up into the air Natalia flew, so high that the crowd lost her for a moment in the clouds.

As Natalia reappeared at the bottom of the clouds, the judge reached down and grabbed a bouquet of yellow and orange flowers. "Release the Candilions," he called and began blowing at the flowers.

Rows of Dancians blew on the Candilions' clocks they had picked from the roadside and the fields. The fiercely protective and fiery tasting flower seeds flew up to meet Natalia and then opened their parachutes to bring her safely to the ground.

"Thank you, my dear ones," Natalia said as she landed and gently blew the red and yellow seeds away.

Many other pole-vaulters jumped, but no one even hit the bottom of the clouds.

Thurin walked back to the tournament from the lake to get ready for the royal joust. He was still drying his hair with a towel when Josef came hopping by, jumping up and down and holding his head between his hands.

"Sooooooo Hottttt," Josef breathed at Thurin. Josef's face was bright red, like a candy apple. His eyes were big and bloodshot. He was sweating so hard that he grabbed Thurin's towel and frantically dabbed his face. "Water," Josef gasped at Thurin. Then Josef took a huge bite out of a red spotted crispy pickle. Josef shoved the towel back at his friend and staggered off, taking crunchy bites of pickle and asking onlookers for water. Thurin laughed as he wrung out his drenched towel. "Finally, Josef is funny! Nobody makes spicy pickles as hot as Mr. Fwaygo."

The third and final day of the tournament arrived. In the bowling green, Sylas and Josef were preparing to bowl against each other. They were the best bowlers in the land. Everyone in all of Dancia knew that either Sir Sylas or Sir Josef would win at hedgehog bowling, they just didn't know which one. Though they were best friends, when it came to bowling, the two were fierce competitors.

HEDGEHOG BOWLING

HEDGEHOGS IN DANCIA LIKE TO BE TICKLED ALMOST AS MUCH AS THEY LIKE TO BE ROLLED. BOWLING PIGEONS ARE NEVER ACTUALLY KNOCKED DOWN, THEY WILL ONLY MOVE IF THEY ARE TOUCHED, AND THEN THEY WILL ONLY FLY A FEW FEET AWAY. BOWLING PIGEONS MOST LIKE SITTING IN ONE PLACE AND BEING FED.

Tickle, tickle, tickle—they tickled their hedgehogs. (This is how you get hedgehogs to roll up into little bowling balls.) Josef and Sylas had taken their places at the lanes in between the hedge trenches when, much to their surprise, Princess Illyana gracefully glided toward them, tickling a hedgehog.

"Uhh, well, hello, uhm Princess . . . " a surprised Sylas stuttered. "What are you doing here? With a hedgehog?"

"Why, I plan to compete, of course!" the princess replied.

"You want to bowl against us? But you're no good at hedgehog bowling," Josef said. "You never have been. We always beat you."

"And perhaps you will again. We'll just have to wait and see, my brave squires," Princess Illyana said mysteriously.

Sylas let loose his hedgehog. Down the green it rolled, and all the bowling pigeons flew away.

"A strike for Sir Sylas," the referee called.

Then Josef let loose his tightly wound, giggling hedgehog. "Nine pigeons for Sir Josef."

"Good shot Josef," Sylas said, "but not good enough."

"Hummmph," a disgruntled Josef grunted.

Now it was Princess Illyana's turn. Nervously, the princess stepped up to the line. She gave her hedgehog an extra little tickle and bowled down the lane.

"A strike for Princess Illyana!" the announcer cried.

"Wow!" Josef and Sylas gasped. "No hedge trencher! Princess, we have never seen you bowl like that. What happened?"

"A lucky lob for the Lady, say I," Josef proclaimed.

The princess looked at the two with an arched eyebrow but said nothing. And so the game continued.

"Eight bowling pigeons for Sir Josef and five for Sir Sylas. Another strike for Princess Illyana," the referee announced.

"This is unprecedented," a not so jolly Josef sputtered.

"Illyana," Sylas said, "Seriously, I don't understand. You used to be such a terrible bowler. You could hardly get your hedgehog down to the bowling pigeons. What changed? "

"Hours and hours and hours of practice, my friends. I have been training early every morning to get better at hedgehog bowling. Yes, I have been practicing," the princess replied, "and I believe I can win."

UNPRECEDENTED:
THIS MEANS THAT IT'S
NEVER HAPPENED BEFORE.

"But you're beating us," Josef cried. "It hardly seems fair. I don't like losing."

"I just wanted to prove that if I practiced really hard, I could get better at something that I've never been very good at," the princess said as she let her hedgehog whirl.

"Strike for the Princess! And that makes her winner of the bowling game!" the referee announced. "Three cheers for Princess Illyana!"

The crowd went wild, cheering for the unexpected winner. The two squires looked at the princess with their mouths wide open.

Hedgehog bowling was the final competition. The tournament was over. In the last three days, new champions were discovered and old ones held their titles. Three new riddle masters were chosen because they answered riddles no one else could. Farmers were given ribbons for their big beautiful fruits and vegetables. Artists and craftsmen were recognized for their skills. The best musicians were awarded the high honor of playing in the orchestra that very night.

Now it was time to prepare for the Grand Ball.

A LONG WINDING STAIR

Up to the top of the central tower in the rock candy palace, then across the delicate, dizzying span of Leap Lightly Bridge, Princess Illyana and her friends walked. Actually, running on the balls of her feet, Illyana skipped and twirled from one friend to another for a quick chat or an encouraging word. Behind the friends came everyone from the tournament that was willing to climb the 2,744 steps to the Grand Ballroom. Of course, Princess Illyana could have called upon the steeds in the Sky Stables to fly everyone to the ballroom. But it was tradition to warm up their legs on the long winding stairway before the Grand Ball.

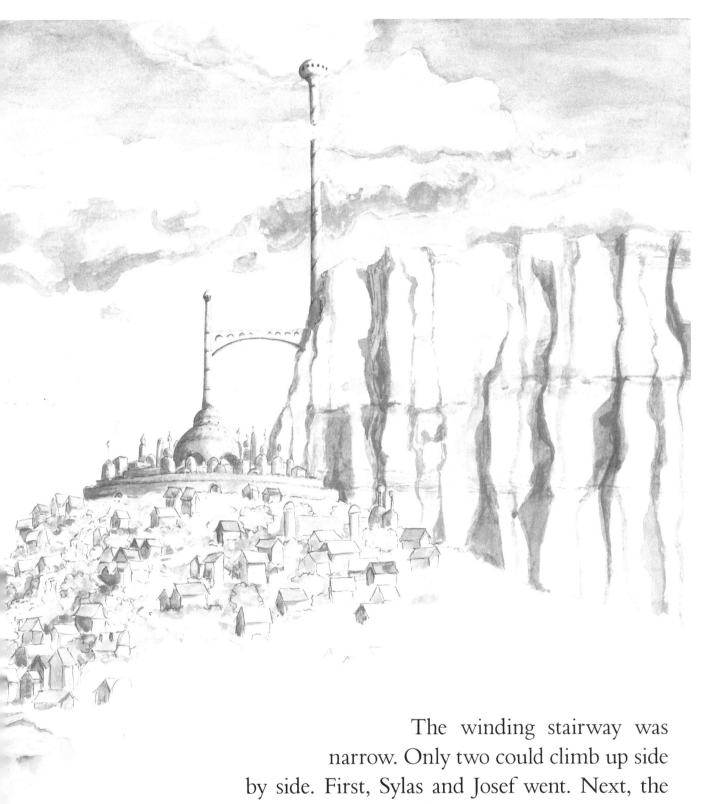

The winding stairway was
narrow. Only two could climb up side
by side. First, Sylas and Josef went. Next, the
ballerina princess and her friend Natalia lightly danced
up the steps. Behind them came Thurin with Brie on his
shoulder chatting into his ear.

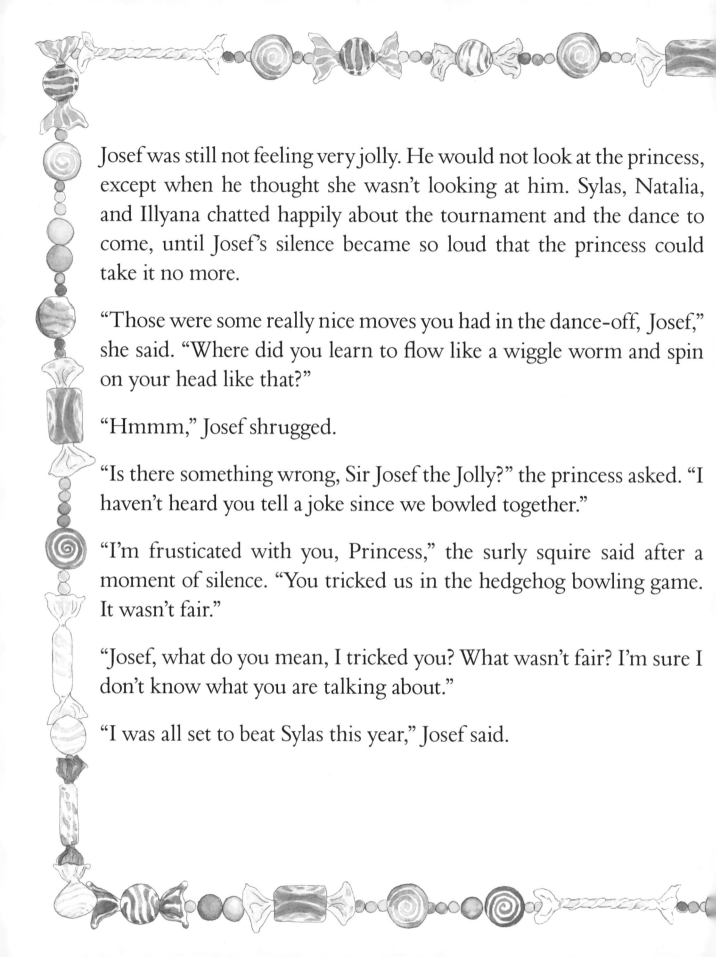

Josef was still not feeling very jolly. He would not look at the princess, except when he thought she wasn't looking at him. Sylas, Natalia, and Illyana chatted happily about the tournament and the dance to come, until Josef's silence became so loud that the princess could take it no more.

"Those were some really nice moves you had in the dance-off, Josef," she said. "Where did you learn to flow like a wiggle worm and spin on your head like that?"

"Hmmm," Josef shrugged.

"Is there something wrong, Sir Josef the Jolly?" the princess asked. "I haven't heard you tell a joke since we bowled together."

"I'm frusticated with you, Princess," the surly squire said after a moment of silence. "You tricked us in the hedgehog bowling game. It wasn't fair."

"Josef, what do you mean, I tricked you? What wasn't fair? I'm sure I don't know what you are talking about."

"I was all set to beat Sylas this year," Josef said.

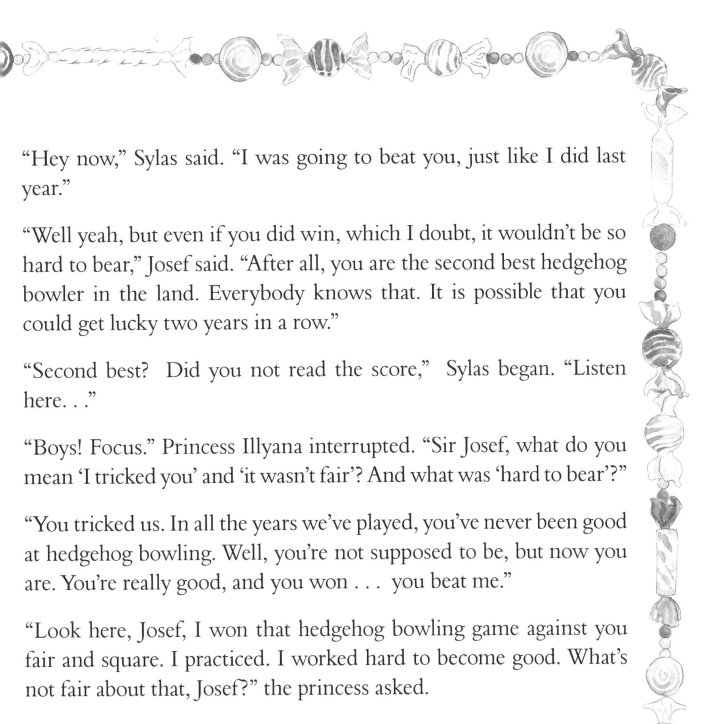

"Hey now," Sylas said. "I was going to beat you, just like I did last year."

"Well yeah, but even if you did win, which I doubt, it wouldn't be so hard to bear," Josef said. "After all, you are the second best hedgehog bowler in the land. Everybody knows that. It is possible that you could get lucky two years in a row."

"Second best? Did you not read the score," Sylas began. "Listen here. . ."

"Boys! Focus." Princess Illyana interrupted. "Sir Josef, what do you mean 'I tricked you' and 'it wasn't fair'? And what was 'hard to bear'?"

"You tricked us. In all the years we've played, you've never been good at hedgehog bowling. Well, you're not supposed to be, but now you are. You're really good, and you won . . . you beat me."

"Look here, Josef, I won that hedgehog bowling game against you fair and square. I practiced. I worked hard to become good. What's not fair about that, Josef?" the princess asked.

Josef didn't answer Princess Illyana. He was walking up the stairs with his hands thrust into his pockets, his shoulders hunched forward, and his eyes glaring at the limestone steps he was climbing.

"Sylas," the princess said. "Do you feel the same way?"

"Hmm, me? I didn't expect you to challenge us at bowling. You can be sure I'll be practicing harder than ever for next year's Tournament. And I certainly didn't expect to lose. That was not my favorite part. But like you said, you beat us fair and square. So I say, "good job Princess," Sylas replied.

"I do have to ask you a question though," Sylas continued. "Why did you want to bowl against us anyway? You've never been interested in it before?"

"I already told you, I wanted to prove that I could be good at whatever I wanted to be good at. I didn't realize it was going to hurt anybody's feelings," the princess said.

"Are there any other reasons, Princess?" Sylas asked.

"I don't know," the princess said, suddenly shy. "Maybe."

"Please tell us," Sylas said.

Now Sir Josef was looking at the princess, his staring contest with the stairs forgotten.

"Well, uhm, it's just that . . . " The normally talkative princess was having trouble speaking.

"What is it Illyana? You can tell us. We're your friends."

"That's just it," the princess stated. "You are my friends. You, Sylas, and Josef, are two great hedgehog bowlers. Both of you have so much fun playing against each other. Natalia, you're an incredible jumper, and Thurin, well, you're just mighty. We are all good at some things and great at others. I wanted to do something that we could all do together, like we used to. Sylas and Josef, when you left your service at the palace last year I really missed you."

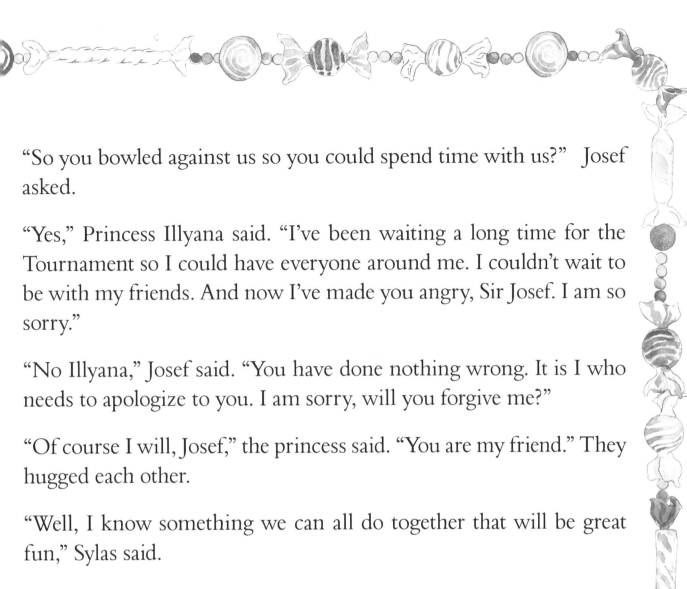

"So you bowled against us so you could spend time with us?" Josef asked.

"Yes," Princess Illyana said. "I've been waiting a long time for the Tournament so I could have everyone around me. I couldn't wait to be with my friends. And now I've made you angry, Sir Josef. I am so sorry."

"No Illyana," Josef said. "You have done nothing wrong. It is I who needs to apologize to you. I am sorry, will you forgive me?"

"Of course I will, Josef," the princess said. "You are my friend." They hugged each other.

"Well, I know something we can all do together that will be great fun," Sylas said.

"What's that, Sylas?" the princess asked.

"We can dance!" Sylas said. From the smiles that lit up everyone's faces, he knew that he had said the right thing.

"On to the ballroom!" Thurin boomed. Up the stairs they went, smiling all the way.

DANCING IN THE SKY

Twilight had touched the air, turning cotton candy clouds pink, red, orange and gold. Up through the clouds rose the rock candy tower turning from pink to purple stone. At last, in the great ballroom at the top of it all, the rock candy turned blue. The ballroom rose above the fiery clouds. It sparkled and floated there like a blue raindrop, as if it were a loving gift from the grateful sky above. Brilliant sunbirds flitted about the vast chamber, lighting the whole room.

A great hush filled the ballroom as everyone assembled in anticipation of Princess Illyana's Saganspin. One by one the Princess's dancers glided out across the floor until they formed a circle. Out came the princess dancing and leaping, prancing and twirling. Then, all the ballerinas joined in the dance— flowing like flowers in wind and sunshine. How beautiful they looked in their purple and yellow gowns. In her pink gown and sparkling jewels, Princess Illyana floated like a cloud on her tippy toes, through the ballerinas.

Dancians young and old began to move back to the farthest walls. Slowly, in the center of the vast chamber, Princess Illyana began to twirl. Faster and faster she spun. Her ballerinas glided toward her. They circled tightly around the princess till she could not be seen. Suddenly, she flew straight up into the air. She came down, and the ballerinas caught her. As they did, they dashed away from her like water droplets. Again, the princess twirled while the ballerinas leapt around her. This water dance celebrated the fountains in the gardens where the Grand Tournament took place.

Now the Dancians watched as the princess and her ballerinas entertained them with the story of the tournament. They charged like horses, flew like arrows, and dropped from the sky—like the young squire who splashed in Deep Water Lake.

They even danced like a naughty horse that moved slowly with a big belly and a carrot in his mouth. When the Saganspin was done, Princess Illyana leapt up to a high place.

"Oohhhh, ahhhh . . . our beautiful princess," the crowd exclaimed.

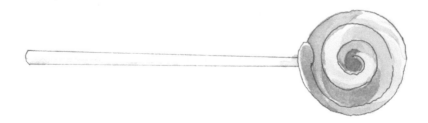

"And now," Princess Illyana cried, "I would like to give out prizes to the tournament winners. To Sir Thurin, with his lungs as mighty as the west wind, for winning the bubble gum blowing contest, I give you a rare and precious seed from the Royal Bubble gum tree. Plant this anywhere you like Thurin, and keep blowing those fantastic bubbles. And for your valorous victory in jousting, I award you a new shield and a sword."

VALOUROUS:
THIS MEANS THAT YOU ARE VERY
COURAGEOUS AND INCLINED TO BE A HERO.

"To Sir Josef, who ate more spicy pickles than anyone else, a year's supply of Mr. Fwaygo's super spicy pickles."

"Oh no," Josef groaned. His face turned red as he remembered just how hot those pickles were. "No more of the Spicy!"

"And also Josef," continued the princess, unaware of her friend's discomfort. "For stepping up your fancy footwork in the dance-off, a brand new pair of tap shoes to begin practicing for your newly awarded role in our winter dance production."

"To Sir Sylas the Speedy, whose aim, like his words and deeds, are always steady and true, I give a new bow for his excellence in the archery competition. And Sylas, I am sorry I had to ground Slowpoke for getting into the Royal Garden and eating all the carrots. I'm sure you'll do very well in the jousting tournament next year, if Slowpoke can behave himself."

"Slowpoke, what did you get into this time?" Sylas said out loud. It was louder than he hoped, for everyone heard it and started laughing. Many were well acquainted with Slowpoke and his antics. The embarrassed squire covered his eyes and shook his head.

"For the beautiful and spry Natalia," called the smiling princess as the laughter quieted. "Whose legendary leaps won her the prize in licorice pole vaulting, your very own soaking tub and cotton candy cloud mattress for all your sore muscles."

"As the host of the tournament I won't award myself anything for winning the hedgehog bowling contest. I will simply say that the satisfaction of hard work and daily practice, then beating the two best hedgehog bowlers in the land, is reward enough for me!"

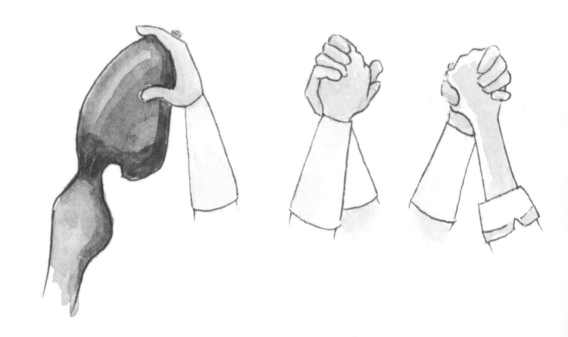

SATISFACTION:
THIS MEANS TO BE FILLED OR CONTENT, HAVING ENOUGH OR BEING HAPPY WITH WHAT YOU HAVE.

"Three cheers for our winners," the kindhearted princess called out. When the cheers subsided, Princess Illyana decreed,

"And now we DANCE!!!"

Sir Sylas twirled his dear friend Princess Illyana speedily around the dance floor. When they were both so dizzy they could spin no more, the princess leapt into Sylas' arms and the strong squire lifted her above his head and carried her around the ballroom.

Knights leapt, and ladies twirled. Even Brie, in an ornate purple vest, danced about the great blue chamber. Music and light and laughter filled the air.

And they danced
the night away,
as Dancians will often do.